Rufus' Great Adventure
(A children's short story)

Rufus' Great Adventure (A children's short story)
Written by Jennifer J. Cole and Frank R. Cole
Edited by Frank R. Cole

Copyright 2021 Frank R. Cole and Jennifer J. Cole
All rights reserved.

Other books by Frank R. Cole:

Discussion From A Beginner Writer, written by Frank R. Cole and Jennifer J. Cole.

Unbounded (A collection of poems), written by Frank R. Cole.

Buckyball (A science fiction screenplay), written by Frank R. Cole.

Drawings by:
(this artist was paid for the drawings presented in this book)
Johny Rood Bongabong

With special thanks to Luche Diamante Cole (wife of Frank R. Cole) who communicated with Johny Rood Bongabong with regards to the drawings.

About the Author
Jennifer J. Cole is a college graduate from Emerson College in Boston, Massachusetts as a B.S. Communications Studies major (2018). She currently (2021) works as a Development Coordinator at Harvard University and attends the Harvard Extension Graduate School for a Master of Arts in Liberal Studies. She is working on a Master's Degree in the area of Sustainability.

Publishing Assistance
This book was recreated from original notes by Jennifer J. Cole that were saved on a computer. The original book was turned in as a school assignment and was never returned. All the original pictures were lost. Dad (Frank R. Cole) took the original notes and added new pictures and drawings to create this book. Some extra pages were added.

Photos
The pictures shown in this story are of Rufus Cole, Jennifer Cole, and brother Anthony Cole.

Dedication

Dedicated to my wonderful dog Rufus who passed away in 2013 at the age of 9. I want to thank my awesome neighbor, "K", who would always take Rufus for walks and who loved Rufus as much as my brother and I did.

About the Story

This story was written in 2007 by Jennifer J. Cole at age 11 as a 6th grade school assignment for a Connecticut Public School. Rufus, a cute little dog, wanders off his yard into places he doesn't know. The story is basically true as one day Rufus' electronic security fence collar fell off him (or he somehow got it off) and Rufus was able to leave the property. Rufus had escaped! Rufus was gone for over a day. The whole family was worried because night came and Rufus was lost. The next day, Mom called the town dog pound and they said they had a dog that fit Rufus' description. Rufus was found. The whole family was so happy. Read and find out all about Rufus' Great Adventure and where he ventures off to.

Rufus is a dog, but not just any dog. He is our family dog and he is very special to us. He has an interesting story to him.

He loves to play and is very cute and friendly.

Rufus causes lots of trouble all around the house and is very mysterious.

He is a Beagle and is almost all black on his back.

Rufus is a small dog with a deep howling voice.

He is very smart and knows the commands for sit, roll over, paw, lay down, fetch, stay, come, and heel.

Rufus loves to hunt out small things underground in the yard.

You could fall in love with Rufus the minute you see him.

He will sit next to you on the couch while you are watching television.

Rufus lets you give him big hugs.

Rufus will be your friend and play with you. He will let you put a Santa Clause hat on him.

In the morning Rufus will jump up on your bed and put his head on your chest while you are waking up.

When you are sad and are hiding under a blanket, Rufus will join you and will stay with you.

He has a long tongue to lick you with.

He will follow you around and stare at you if you are eating food.

It is hard to resist Rufus' big eyes when he is staring at you.

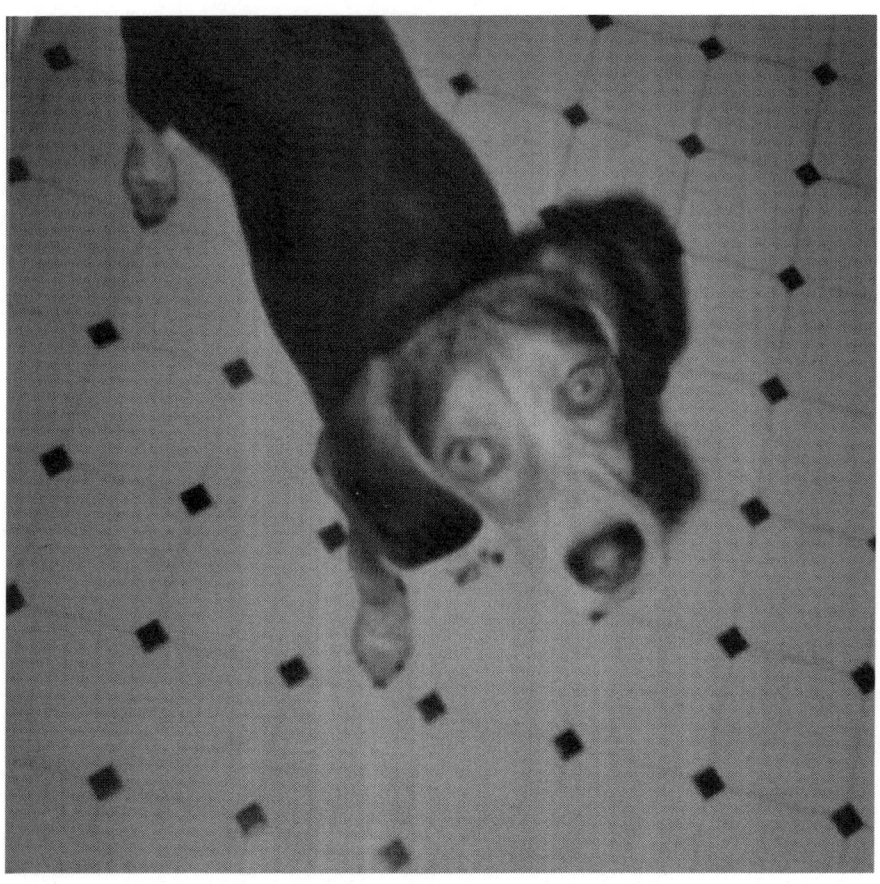

Rufus is helpful for finding run away hamsters that hide in small places.

He chews on many things like shoes, stuffed animals, plastic, and loves to tear open the garbage.

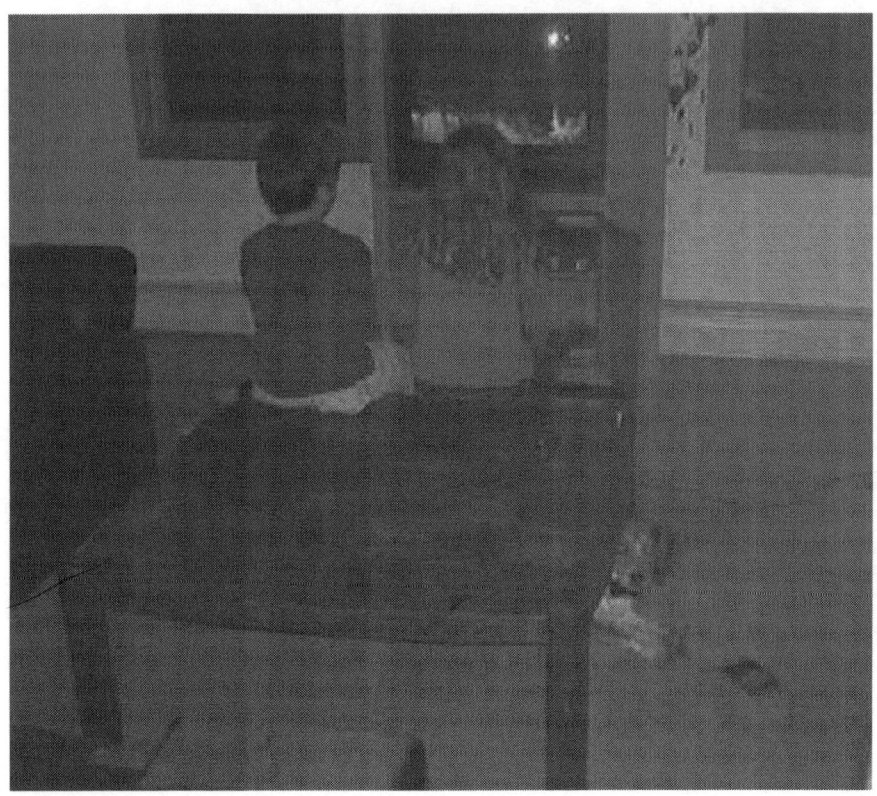

Rufus is very picky about what he eats; he won't eat vegetables or bread.

Rufus is a gentle Beagle that you would love to meet!

Mom had to get Rufus the biggest electric fence collar they made because the smaller collars did not stop Rufus from leaving the yard.

One day, Rufus was in his own yard doing his own business and he realized that his collar was not on.

He took advantage of this and ran off the yard in a scurry, up the driveway, and onto the street at about 12:00 in the afternoon.

Rufus, being free of the yard, was happily prancing down the street sniffing new sniffs.

The neighborhood was very friendly and everybody knew everybody. If someone saw Rufus, they would have brought him home, but everybody on the street was at the big carnival on the green that day!

Luckily this street did not have many cars on it. Usually a car would come down the street only once every hour. This was because the street had a cul-de-sac and there were only about ten houses on the street.

When Rufus got to the end of the street, he saw a path that led to the woods and Rufus did not know if he should go in.

The woods were deep, dark, scary, and full of bugs.

All of a sudden Rufus heard noises from all the way in the back of the woods.

They sounded like animal noises. The noises sounded like neighs from horses, oinks from pigs, moos from cows, and baaks from chickens.

These noises attracted Rufus far into the woods.

When he got to the other side of the woods, there were many rows of tall, skinny stalks which were corn plants. There was a big red house and fenced areas with animals inside them. Where do you think Rufus was?

Well, Rufus did not really care, he just went wherever his nose took him.

Rufus' nose smelled a very strong scent and he followed it barking and wagging his tail.

This scent took him out of the corn field and into a pig pen.

There were pigs in the pen and the pigs got very disturbed when they saw Rufus because they did not know who Rufus was.

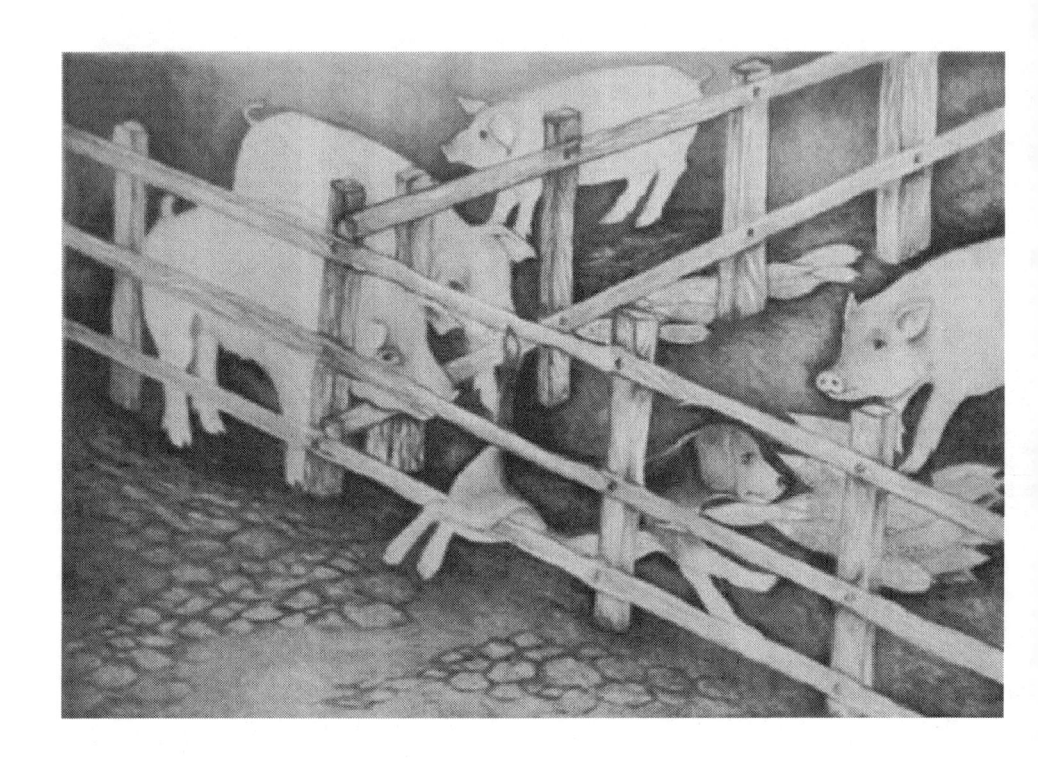

Rufus was a very friendly dog and he thought everybody and everything was friendly. So, Rufus invited himself into the pig pen.

Rufus also smelled food in the pig pen and that was the main reason he wanted to go in. Rufus was always following his nose especially if there was the smell of food.

Rufus did not really mind the pigs and he rolled in the mud with them and ate their food.

Rufus was fine up to the point where one of the pigs decided it did not like Rufus in the pig pen. The pig began to chase Rufus. Rufus was smart enough to know when he was not wanted, so Rufus dashed out of the pig pen frightened of the big pig coming at him.

After being chased by the pig, Rufus learned a lesson and was more cautious about where he followed his nose.

Rufus saw a big red barn and decided that he wanted to go there because he was hungry and thirsty and he thought there might be some food and water there.

So he pranced on over to the big red barn and noticed that there were big doors. Rufus went inside the big barn doors. Once inside, Rufus saw a bunch of hay on the ground, he saw a big tin of water, and he saw a brush.

By this time in Rufus' journey, Rufus was very tired and he needed a nap, so he lied down on a big pile of hay and fell asleep.

Minutes later, Rufus woke up startled to hear – "Neigh, Neigh!". Rufus noticed that there was a big horse in the stall where he had fallen asleep. The horse was on its back legs questioning what Rufus was doing in its stall.

Rufus was so frightened that he started to cry.

When the barn lady realized that something wrong was going on, she came out of her office and got Rufus out of there as fast as she could, and then calmed her horse down.

After that big commotion, the barn lady took Rufus back to her office and was about to lock him in the office so he would not get away. She wanted to feed Rufus and find his owner.

But before she got a chance to close the door, Rufus dashed out of the office and then ran out of the barn.

The barn lady was chasing Rufus for a while trying to catch him. But she could not catch Rufus because he was too fast for her.

Rufus kept running and running until he stopped to take a break by a big tree in the forest.

Rufus was trying to fall asleep by the big tree but was too distracted by all the other noises around him. A forest squirrel was squeaking.

As Rufus kept walking in the forest, he came upon a creek. The creek was not deep. Rufus looked into the creek and saw fish swimming in the water.

Rufus had seen creeks before in the forest when he took walks with his family. Rufus was smart enough to know where the creek was not deep and so Rufus started crossing the creek to the other side.

While Rufus was in the middle of the creek, he looked upstream and then he looked downstream. Rufus wondered where those led to and if he should follow in those directions. Rufus crossed the creek and smelled something downstream.

After Rufus crossed the creek, he followed his nose downstream. Rufus saw another animal eating berries from a bushy tree. It was a deer. The deer had antlers.

Rufus tried to be quiet while he was watching the deer eat the berries. Suddenly the deer stopped eating berries and looked right at Rufus.

The deer did not like Rufus watching. The deer flicked one ear and then bounded away out of sight. As the deer bounded away all Rufus could see was the white tail of the deer as it disappeared into the forest.

Rufus followed his nose downstream. As Rufus went further downstream, the stream got wider and deeper.

After a while, Rufus came to the entrance of a State Park. There was a sign. Rufus' nose told him that he had been here before with his family. Rufus followed his nose along the trail.

The trail that Rufus had been following led to an overlook canyon. Rufus' nose told him it was dangerous to get too close to the edge. Rufus kept following the stream.

A short distance further ahead, the stream met the cliffs. There was a beautiful waterfall. Rufus had been here before with his family. Rufus smelled the air to tell if his family were there. Rufus' nose told him that his family was not there and that he was getting far from home. Rufus turned around and went back upstream.

Rufus followed the trail back upstream. There were many paths that led to different places, but Rufus followed his nose.

One noise stood out to Rufus, it was the voice of children. Rufus thought it was his family, so he went to check it out.

Rufus went over to the noise and saw three little boys about five to nine years old on bicycles. They were riding bicycles on the street.

These boys were not Rufus' family but the boys looked friendly, so Rufus thought that he could have some fun with them. Rufus went over to the boys and followed them as they rode their bicycles. Rufus was looking as cute as possible.

The boys noticed the cute little dog and they started playing with Rufus. They petted Rufus and ran around with him.

The boys were all brothers and they were playing outside their house. Their mom was watching them from the window and got worried about this strange dog that her boys were playing with.

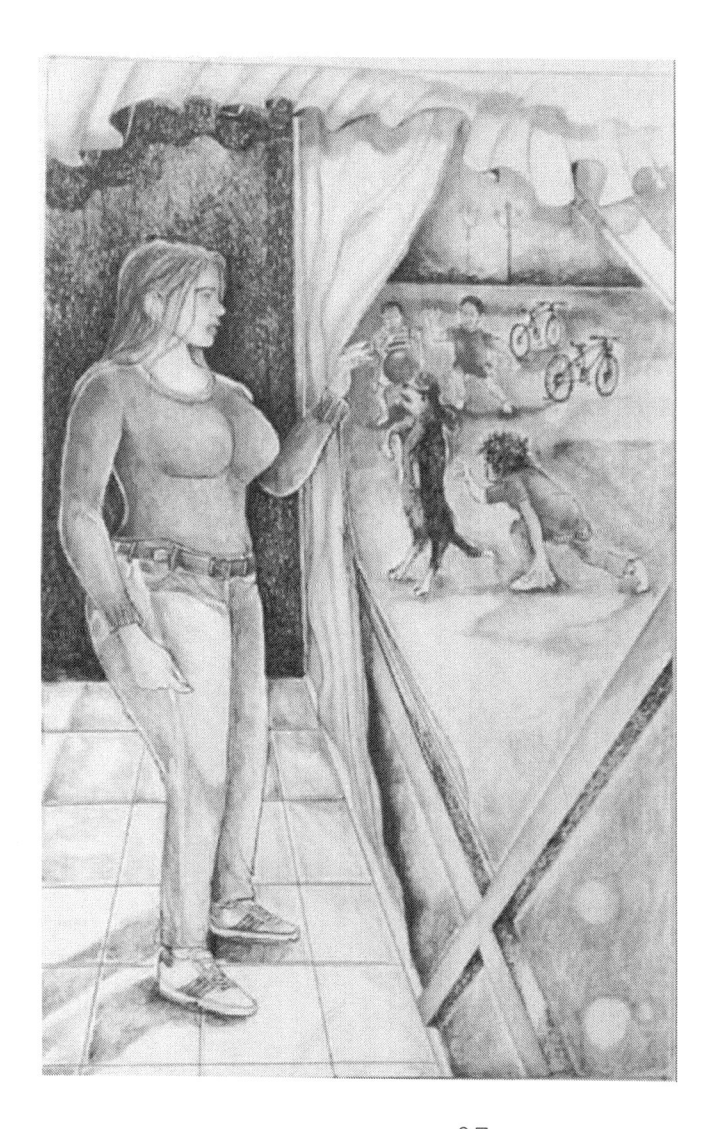

The mom came outside and asked her children what they were doing with the strange dog.

The mom did not see a collar on Rufus, as it had fallen off before he ran away from home. The mom thought Rufus was either a lost dog or a stray dog.

The mom decided to trick Rufus in order to catch him. She got a piece of ham and waved it in the air. Rufus came right to her when he smelled that ham because he was very hungry. The mom was able to put a collar around Rufus. She tied Rufus up and called the dog pound right away. She did not want a strange dog in her neighborhood.

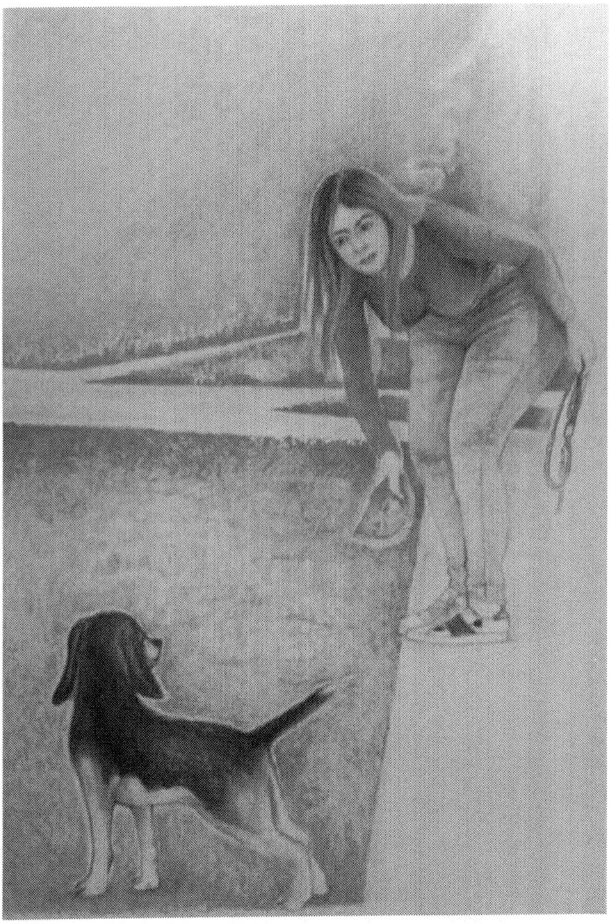

The dog pound officer came right away in a big truck. Rufus was very scared going into the big truck. He did not know where he was going or what was going to happen to him.

When Rufus got to the dog pound, they locked him in a cage and walked away.

The dog pound guard liked Rufus a lot and would give Rufus a snack every time that Rufus looked sad.

As it got dark, Rufus' family realized that Rufus was missing. They searched the yard for Rufus. They found Rufus's dog collar on the ground.

They searched the neighborhood calling for Rufus. Rufus was nowhere to be found!

Mom called around to find Rufus. Nobody had seen Rufus. He was lost. Rufus' family hoped that Rufus was not hurt. Mom called the dog pound but they were closed. It was a very sad night that night without Rufus in the house.

It was hard for Rufus to sleep that night. He was in a strange place and there was barking and howling by the other dogs all night long. Rufus had a very sad night at the dog pound. Rufus missed his family.

Rufus dreamed of being free of the dog pound jail. He dreamed of being in the woods with the squirrels and birds that he saw that day.

The next morning Rufus' mom called the dog pound again and they told her he was there. Rufus' family went right away to pick Rufus up from the dog pound.

When Rufus' family arrived, Rufus smelled them and he howled and cried with happiness. Rufus and his family went home together, all feeling very happy that they were together again.

After that day, Rufus learned his lesson from his great adventure. He learned how to escape from the yard. He learned what was beyond his yard. He learned that he did not like being locked up in the dog pound.

Rufus would escape from the yard many times after that first great adventure but he always returned home before dark.

Rufus, the smart little dog, was never caught again.

And lastly, Rufus, after his great adventure, after figuring out how to escape from his electric fence, after wandering down his street, after exploring the farm, after following his nose through the woods, after exploring the state park, after playing with the three boys, after being locked in the dog pound jail, and after being picked up by his family finally learned his greatest lesson that with all the marvelous things in the world the best place to follow your nose is to follow your nose home to your family.

The End

Anthony and Jennifer Cole

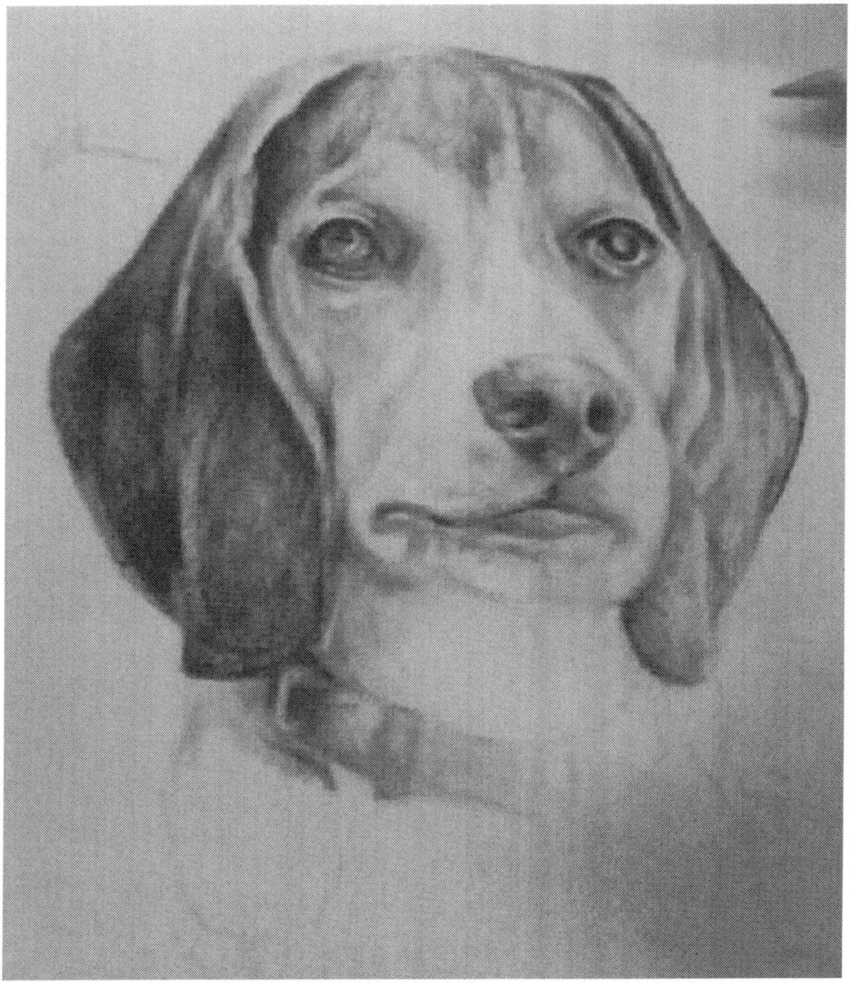

Made in the USA
Coppell, TX
29 March 2021

52621785R10070